P9-CED-586

THE THREE PIGS

DAVID WIESNER

SCHOLASTIC INC.
New York Toronto London Auckland Sydney
Mexico City New Delhi Hong Kong Buenos Aires

To David Macaulay

&

To Carol Goldenberg

with gratitude

And special thanks to Andi Stern

ISBN 0-439-44517-5

Published by Scholastic Inc., 557 Broadway, New York,
NY 10012, by arrangement with Clarion Books.

12 11 10 9 8 7 6 5 4 3 2 2 3 4 5 6 7/0

Printed in Mexico 49

First Scholastic printing, September 2002
The artwork was executed in watercolor, gouache,
colored inks, pencil, and colored pencil on Fabriano hot press paper.
The text was set in 17.5 point New Century Schoolbook and
16-point Benguiat Book (and in manipulated forms of these faces),
18-point Tekton, and 42-point Dom Casual.
Art direction and typography by Carol Goldenberg.

Once upon a time there were three pigs who went out into the world to seek their fortune. The first pig decided to build a house, and he built it out of straw.

Along came a wolf, who knocked at the door and said, “Little pig, little pig, let me come in.”

And the pig answered, “Not by the hair of my chinny-chin-chin.”

The wolf said, “Then I’ll huff and I’ll puff and I’ll blow your house in!”

So the wolf huffed, and he puffed, and he blew the house in . . .
Hey! He blew me right out of the story!
. . . and ate the pig up.

Now, the second pig built his house out of sticks. Along came the wolf, who knocked at the door and said, "Little pig, little pig, let me come in."

And the pig answered, “Not by the hair of my chinny-chin-chin.”
The wolf said, “Then I’ll huff and I’ll puff and I’ll blow your house in!”
Come on—it’s safe out here.
So the wolf huffed, and he puffed, and he blew the house in . . . and ate the pig up.

Along came a wolf, who
the door and said, "Little pig,
let me come in."
The third pig built his house out of bricks.
We got away from that wolf . . . for good.
Wow! Why didn't you two get eaten up?

And the pig answered, "Not by the hair of my chinny-chin-chin."
The wolf said, "Then I'll huff and I'll puff and I'll blow your house in!"
Now we have room to move. Watch this— oops!

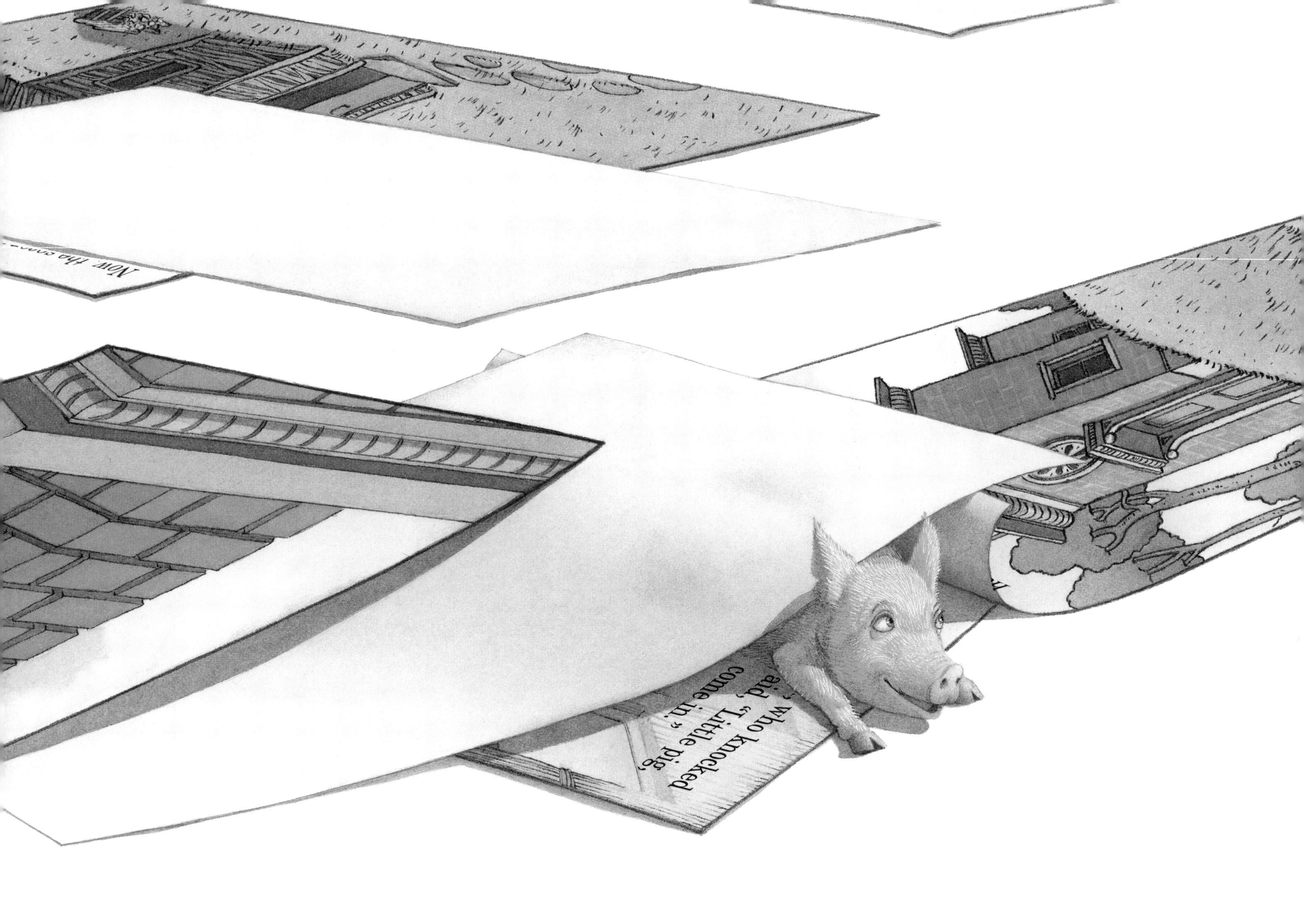
Now the
who knocked
aid, "Little pig,
come in."

Let's explore this place.
OK. Just let me fold this up . . .
te the pig up.

Wheeeeeee!

Uh-oh.

who knocked
“Little pig

Ooof!
Hey!
Over here!
Wait—
what's that?

I think . . .
someone's out
there.

Come help us with this.

Hey
diddle diddle,
The cat and the fiddle,
The cow jumped
over the moon.

The little dog
laughed to see such sport,
And the dish ran away
with the spoon.
Let's get
out of here!

cat
Whew! Where to?

e echidna
f fish
How about in here—oops!
This one. Come on.
High on a hill the
guard over a

High on a hill there lived a great dragon, who stood guard over a rose made of the purest gold.

The king was determined to own this treasure. So he
sent his eldest son to slay the dragon and bring
back the golden rose.
Come with us
—hurry!

The prince spurred his steed to the mountaintop, drew his sword, and slew the mighty dragon.

Many thanks for rescuing me, O brave and noble swine.
Don't mention it.
Hey diddle diddle!
Look who's here. Welcome!

Find something?
What is this?
Now what?

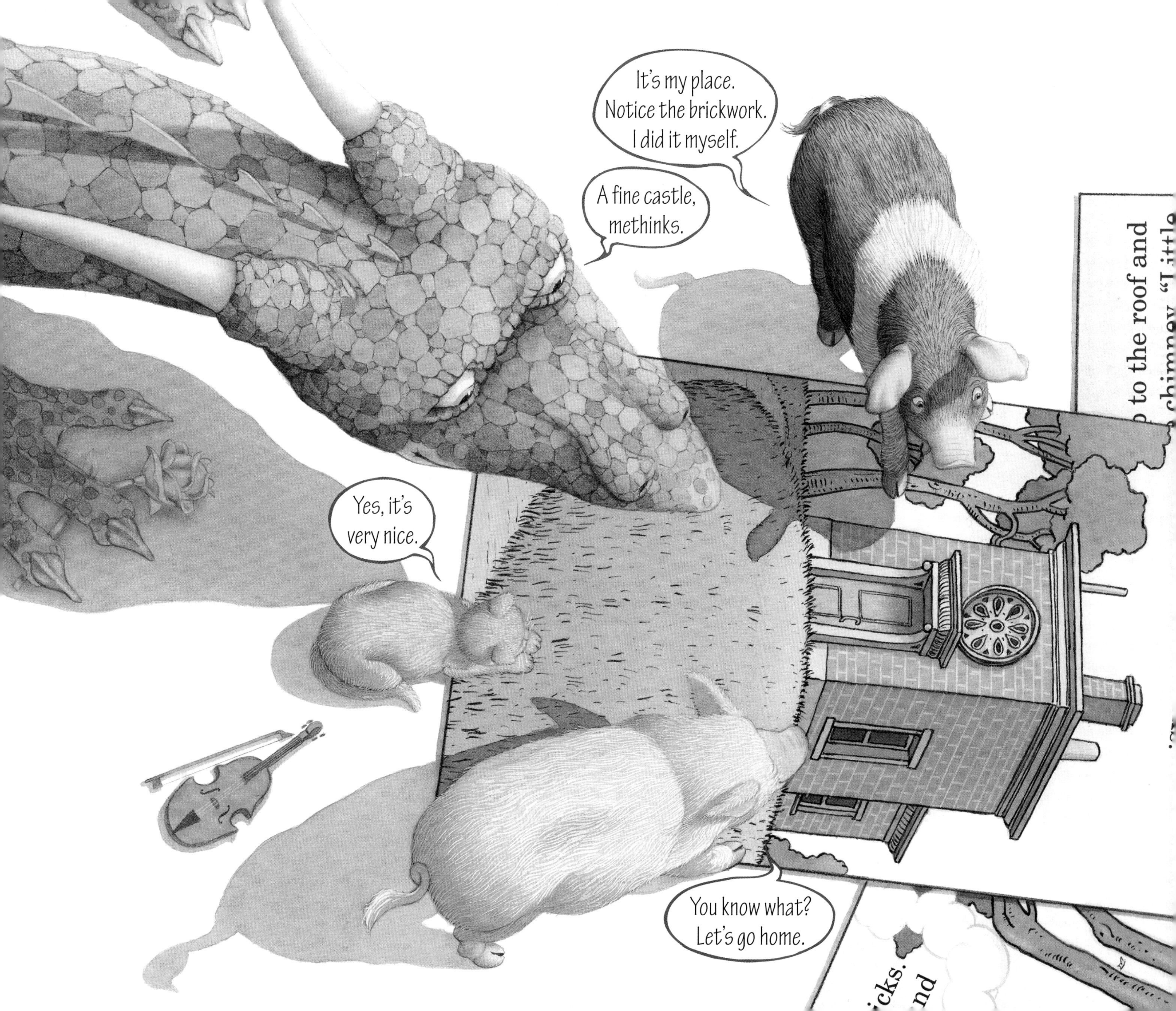

It's my place. Notice the brickwork. I did it myself.
A fine castle, methinks.
Yes, it's very nice.
You know what? Let's go home.

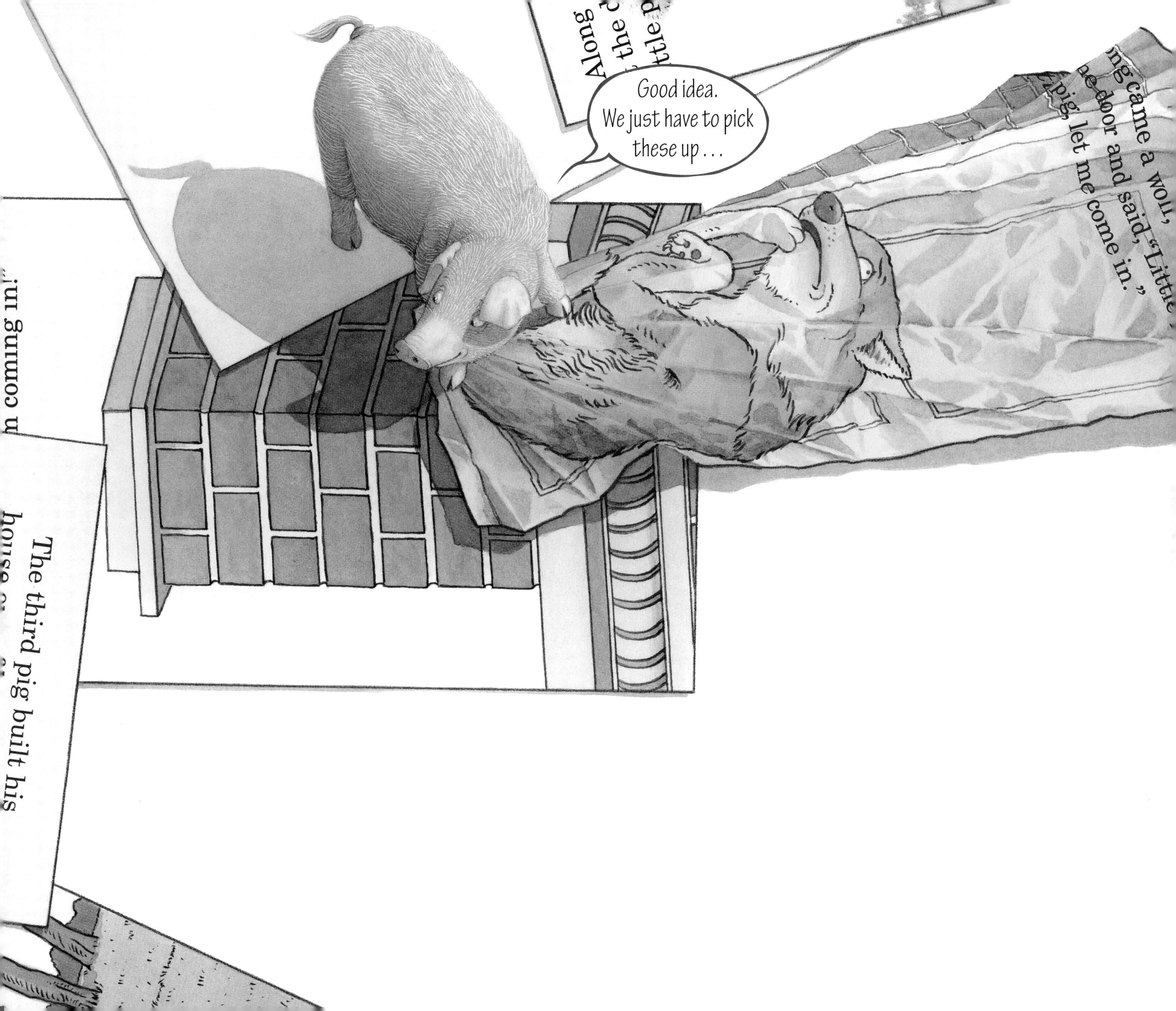
Good idea.
We just have to pick
these up . . .
The third pig built his

hird pig built his
ut of bricks.
Along came a wolf, who knocked
at the door and said, “Little pig,
little pig, let me come in.”

And the pig answered, “Not by the hair of my chinny-chin-chin.”

The wolf said, “Then I’ll huff and I’ll puff and I’ll blow your house in!”

The wolf huffed, and he
But no matter how much
could not blow down

So he clim
OK, that's enough!
Come inside, everyone. Soup's on!
I think we're going to like it here.

And they all lived happily
ever aft